Bear Can't Sleep!

Marni McGee

Sean Julian

LITTLE TIGER PRESS
London

It was winter and all the animals were busy. Soon the forest would be covered in snow.

Fox gathered wood for winter fires while Owl and Squirrel made pickles and jam.

Patch the Hare tried to help, but he got in everyone's way – as usual.

whoops!

"Oh, get your feet
out of my berries!"
cried Squirrel.

"Hush," hooted Owl.
"What's that strange sound?"

Peeping around the trees, the animals saw a huge, grumbly bear dragging branches behind him.

Everyone froze, except Patch.

"Hey, Mr Bear!" he shouted.
"Need some help?"

He's as big as a mountain.

He's heading for the cave!

"Leave me BE!"
snapped the bear.
"I need to SLEEP!"
And he shuffled
into the cave.

Suddenly, his scooter hit a rock.

CRASH!

Down he tumbled, right on top of the blueberry and onion sandwiches.

SPLAT!

From inside the cave came a terrible roar.

"Be QUIET out there,"
Bear bellowed. "Or ELSE!"

"Eeeek," squealed Mouse.
"He's coming to get us!"
"Quick!" cried Owl. "Hide!"

All the animals hid – except Patch,
who picked up one not-so-squashed sandwich
and walked right up to the
dark cave.

"Come back here, Hare!"
Fox called.

But Patch tiptoed closer . . .

As Patch peeked in, he heard Bear sigh:
"I'm old and I'm cold. I'm too shiver-cold to sleep."

"He's not hungry," Patch whispered.
"He's cold. Oh poor old bear!"

All day long, Patch couldn't stop worrying about Bear.

Finally he lay down under a tree to think. As he looked,

the leaves made a patchwork against the evening sky.

And Patch had an idea!

zzz

That night
he tiptoed through
the forest . . .

snore

borrowing things
from all the animals.

Patch **pinned** and **stitched** till dawn.

When the animals woke,
they were **hopping mad.**

Just then, Patch appeared.
He spread a beautiful
patchwork quilt
on the ground.

My pyjamas!

Suddenly **Bear** stomped into the clearing.
He lifted Fox into the air.

"I SAID be QUIET," he roared.
"I'm TRYING to SLEEP!"

The animals shook with fear –
except Patch, of course.

Patch jumped onto a stump.

"Don't be cross, Mr Bear," he begged.

"We brought you a present – look!

It's made from clothes borrowed
from all the animals."

The old bear sniffed, then
gently set Fox down.

"You gave your things...to me?" he said.
"What fine friends you are!"

He made a quilt.

To keep you warm.

Bear clutched the cosy quilt to his furry chest,
and shuffled back into the cave.

"Hey, Mr Bear," called Patch. "How about some
bedtime stories?"

And so, as the first flakes of snow drifted
down, the animals snuggled together
and told stories until

Bear fell

fast

asleep.